THE PRINCESS OF THE SEA

Arthur Gordon

'Arthur Gordon'

BRIXHAM.

ARTHUR H. STOCKWELL LTD
Torrs Park, Ilfracombe, Devon, EX34 8BA
Established 1898
www.ahstockwell.co.uk

British Library Cataloguing-in-Publication Data.
A catalogue record for this book is available
from the British Library.

ISBN 978-0-7223-4992-2
Printed in Great Britain by
Arthur H. Stockwell Ltd
Torrs Park   Ilfracombe
Devon EX34 8BA

CONTENTS

Preface   5
Chapter 1   The Mewstone   9
Chapter 2   Neighbours   15
Chapter 3   A Meeting of Old Friends   18
Chapter 4   Spring-Cleaning   22
Chapter 5   A Traveller of the Oceans   25
Chapter 6   A Gathering   29
Chapter 7   A Holiday Invitation   32
Chapter 8   Thatcher Rock   34
Chapter 9   Preparations   40
Chapter 10   Summer Ball   42

THE PRINCESS OF THE SEA

PREFACE

This is a story about the Princess of the Sea, Miranda, a beautiful mermaid who lives in a cave at the Mewstone on the coast of South Devon. The story tells of her adventures and friends who live with her in the sea.

The Princess of the Sea has many friends of all shapes and sizes. Neptune is the leader of the seahorses that reside in the seagrass beds near Torquay. Herman, a hermit crab, is one of her nearest neighbours. Dolly and Devon, a dolphin and her calf, are frequent visitors. Occasionally, she meets up with the mighty Bertram, a blue whale, the largest mammal on earth.

Miranda is concerned about pollution in the sea and she organises the hundreds of crabs that live at the bottom of the sea to improve the marine environment. Working together, the crabs collect the plastic rubbish and carry it to the beach, where it is washed back up on to dry land. Similarly, she meets with the grey seals and helps to resolve their concerns regarding overfishing in inshore waters and the depletion of fish stocks.

Miranda and the other characters in this book are of course fictitious. However, the places described are very real. The Mewstone, Thatcher Rock, Berry Head and Blackpool Sands are all actual places in South Devon.

I hope that the combination of fictional characters set against the background of real places is of interest to readers and encourages them to come and visit this beautiful part of our island.

Literature is all about imagination and storytelling. I very much hope that young readers enjoy my endeavours.

This is my first novel and I am delighted that Arthur H. Stockwell Ltd has offered publication.

Finally, I must express my gratitude to my new colleague, Miss Tara Prudden, for the artistic contribution in her beautiful illustrations which bring the characters to life.

Best wishes,

Arthur Gordon

THE PRINCESS OF THE SEA

The Princess of the Sea
brushes her hair of gold, soft and long;
she swims in the waters, wild and free.
On sunny summer days she often sings a song.

Miranda loves the sea and the endless blue sky.
Her eyes are crystal blue and her skin is fair.
She watches the boats as they slowly sail by –
a lady of great beauty, without a care.

Her hair is golden, the colour of sunrise.
She lives at the Mewstone, quite near the shore.
Miranda always has laughter in her eyes –
she is a mythical lady of Devon folklore.

CHAPTER 1

THE MEWSTONE

She dived down deep under the water in the choppy sea and swam down to the entrance to her watery cave at the bottom of the rock. She then gently swam up the steep stone stairs. The stairs were about 100 feet high and deep under the sea. They led to a large dry cave, her seaside home. The sea could never rise above the top of the stairs, and then she was on dry land. She crossed the hallway and picked up a towel in the bathroom to dry her hair.

She lived in a magical cave inside the Mewstone. The Mewstone is a large outcrop of rock rising out of the sea just offshore, near Dartmouth in Devon. Her home was just like an ordinary small cottage, except that it was inside a cave. She had an entrance hallway at the top of the stairs, where the sea ended. This led into her kitchen and parlour, where she received visitors. She also had a bedroom, a spare bedroom and a bathroom. It was cosy in her underwater world; it was nice and dry and she had her home comforts.

Princess Miranda was a mermaid – a beautiful lady of the sea. She was not very tall and she had long golden blonde hair. She liked to brush her hair to keep it clean and shining. Her eyes were sparkling crystal blue and bright. The lower half of her was traditional mermaid with emerald-green and gold fish scales ending in her large whale tail.

Her whale tail, or fluke, was used to propel her through the water and she also used it for balance. Princess Miranda was a wonderful swimmer and she could easily power her way through the cold sea even if the weather was stormy and the tide and current were against her.

Miranda lived on her own on the isolated Mewstone. However, she was not lonely – she had lots of visitors and she met up with her friends in the sea every day. She was friends with all the local grey seals. Some seals lived on a flat platform of rock at the base of the Mewstone; others lived in the nearby River Dart and in the harbour at the port of Brixham.

Suddenly, she heard the call of a grey seal coming from her hallway. She moved down the hallway to meet the visitor.

'Hello, Your Ladyship,' said Sam, the grey seal.

'Please come in,' replied Princess Miranda. 'It's great to see you.'

Sam shuffled along the hallway with Miranda into the parlour. Sam lived on the Mewstone with his partner, Mary, and their young seal pup named Sheba. Sam was the leader of the grey-seal colony in South Devon. He was Miranda's

nearest neighbour and he was also her ambassador. He always accompanied her on formal occasions and he always spoke to Miranda with the greatest of respect.

'I've come to tell Your Ladyship that yesterday Gina gave birth to a beautiful male pup. Mother and pup are doing very well.'

'What wonderful news!' said Miranda. 'We shall go and visit them tomorrow. We can swim over to Brixham at high tide at about eleven o'clock.'

'It will be a pleasure to accompany you as always,' replied Sam.

Sam then took his leave from the Princess and joined Mary and little Sheba on the rock. They lived on a flat platform of rock at one side of the Mewstone. Seals have a thick hide and deep layers of blubber, which protect them from the cold of the sea and the marine environment. They are quite happy living at the Mewstone.

The following day Sam called upon Miranda and together they swam in the sea to Brixham. Gina was lying on the beach at Churston Cove, an isolated cove, gently cuddling her newborn pup. The pup was a bundle of thick yellow fur with two eyes as black as coal. They all exchanged greetings and Sam gave Gina a present of some fresh mackerel.

'Thank you, Sam, and it is lovely to see you, Your Ladyship,' replied Gina. She looked at her newborn pup and sighed. 'I

hope he will become a big strong fisherman, just like his father.'

They all kissed and said their goodbyes, and Sam escorted Princess Miranda back to her home at the Mewstone.

CHAPTER 2

NEIGHBOURS

It was late in the month of May and summer had arrived. The sun shone brightly in the sky and the waters sparkled in the intense sunlight. The waters around South Devon were now teeming with shoals of fish: mackerel, bream, bass and pollock.

Miranda sidled down her stairs and dived into the water. She was in search of some breakfast. As she swam along the bottom of the sea she heard a voice.

'Good morning, Your Ladyship,' said Herman.

'And a very good morning to you,' replied Miranda.

Herman was a hermit crab and one of Miranda's neighbours. He lived underneath a rock near the Mewstone. He sheltered by the rock and lived on morsels of food swept there by the currents of the sea. Unlike a common crab, Herman lived inside a very thick pink seashell and he liked to live alone. It was early summer and the seawater was beginning to warm up. The waters were teeming with fish and newly laid fish spawn, so there was plenty of food for Herman.

'When you see Gina, please pass on my congratulations to her on her newborn pup,' said Herman.

'How did you know about it?' replied Miranda.

'Sam told me. He keeps me up to date on all the gossip,' replied Herman.

They said goodbye to each other and Miranda continued with her morning swim. Herman remained by the rock, constantly on the lookout for passing tasty morsels.

Miranda continued to forage on the sea floor and she went to view an ancient shipwreck. The wreck was of a Spanish galleon. There were few remains apart from part of the wooden hull and a few cannons covered in barnacles.

As she approached the wreck she heard a voice.

'Hello, Your Ladyship. I was wondering if you would pay me a visit,' said Ernie.

'Oh, hello, Ernie. How are you keeping?' replied Miranda.

'I am well, thank you. I envy you living in your huge cave at the Mewstone. I wish I could afford to go upmarket instead of living in this old shipwreck,' replied Ernie.

'Yes, but you are well hidden and you eat very well,' said Miranda.

'That's true and there are plenty of fish around the wreck,' replied Ernie.

Ernie was an old slimy conger eel. He was pleasant most of the time, but on occasions he could be cantankerous. They exchanged goodbyes and Miranda headed back home.

CHAPTER 3

A MEETING OF OLD FRIENDS

It was a wonderful summer morning and Miranda sat in front of the mirror with her head to one side, brushing her hair. She sipped her morning tea and listened to the sound of the sea and the swirling waters in her home under the sea.

She decided to venture further afield this day, and she began swimming out to sea in the clear blue waters in Start Bay on the coast of South Devon. She swam to the surface of the sea and she could see lots of sailing boats pounding through the swell with a moderate easterly wind in their sails. It was mid-morning and the sun was high in the sky and the waters sparkled in the sun. Flocks of seagulls patrolled the skies and dived into the sea in their endless hunt for fish. In the distance on the rocky shore a group of cormorants were perched with their wings outstretched, drying in the hot morning sun.

Presently, she was in deep water a few miles offshore.

She then heard an enormous splash near her and the sound of laughter.

'Good morning, Your Ladyship,' said Dolly.

'Oh, you startled me, Dolly,' replied Miranda.

Dolly was accompanied by her little calf, sheltered by her side, and they were doing their usual morning swim in the sea. Dolly was a bottlenose dolphin.

'I love your calf. Have you thought of a name yet?' asked Miranda.

'I love him immensely, Your Ladyship. I have decided to call him Devon because we live mainly in the seas around Devon, and it is a very beautiful place.'

'I think that is a lovely name for him,' replied Miranda.

'Thank you. We have just come from the Skerries Bank, and the mackerel fishing there has been excellent,' said Dolly.

The Skerries Bank is a large area of sandbanks just off Slapton Sands on the South Devon coast. The waters there are shallow and it is well known for the gathering of large shoals of fish.

'I have been on one of my usual outings across Start Bay. I will now head back home to the Mewstone,' said Miranda.

'It's always a pleasure to meet you, Your Ladyship. And enjoy the sunshine,' said Dolly.

With the arrival of summer, the sea had warmed up. It was now early afternoon and the Princess of the Sea slowly

made her way back home. The tide was now in her favour and she did not have to swim hard to move through the water.

As a mermaid Miranda had many duties to carry out. When she was swimming in the sea she always kept an eye out for passing ships and their crews. If ever a member of a ship's crew fell overboard she would be on hand to effect a rescue.

CHAPTER 4

SPRING-CLEANING

The warm summer weather continued and the days were long. At night it hardly seemed to get dark. Miranda enjoyed living in her cave at the bottom of the sea – it was quiet, but she enjoyed the peace and solitude.

It was now time to do some housekeeping. She had already spoken with Colin, her neighbour, and she would address the assembled crowd later that day. Colin was a common crab, and at the request of the Princess of the Sea he had called a meeting of all the crabs that lived in the coastal waters of South Devon.

On a balmy summer evening the crabs had all gathered near the Mewstone in South Devon.

Sam, the grey seal, chaperoned the Princess of the Sea to the meeting. Sam gave the introduction and then Miranda rose to give her speech.

'Good evening, ladies and gentlemen, and thank you for coming. It is that time of year again when I must ask you to do your duty and clean up all of the rubbish that has gathered on the sea floor. I suggest you work in groups and gather up all of the plastic cups and bags, etc., and carry them to the seashore for mankind to collect. The plastic is not of your making and it has to be returned to those who put it in our sea.'

All of the crabs clapped their claws in appreciation of her speech.

The following day the crabs picked up the plastic cups and plastic bags in their claws and headed to the beach. They dropped the rubbish as close as possible to the seashore. The wind and tide would wash all of the rubbish up on to the beach. People who lived in the villages and towns by the sea would then collect the rubbish.

As Princess of the Sea, Miranda had lots of duties to perform. Once every three months she called upon the services of the crabs to keep the sea free from all of the litter that gathered. It was an endless task, but necessary in order to control pollution.

CHAPTER 5

A TRAVELLER OF THE OCEANS

Miranda was at home sharing afternoon tea with her neighbour Sam. It was a peaceful summer afternoon and they enjoyed sharing the local gossip. Gina and her little seal pup were thriving. The pup had put on a lot of weight and his fur coat was gradually being replaced with a grey coat, common to all seals.

'I heard a deep bellow the other day,' said Miranda. 'I'm sure a whale is approaching our area.'

'Yes, I heard him too, Your Ladyship,' said Sam. 'I think it was old Bertram.'

'I agree with you. Tomorrow we will swim out to Berry Head and keep an eye out for him,' replied Miranda.

The following day Miranda and Sam met on the rocky platform of the Mewstone. The previous evening they had both again heard the distant bellow of a creature from the ocean. It was a perfect summer's day and the sea was calm. Together they dived into the water and swam in a north-easterly direction towards the cliffs at Berry Head.

Berry Head is an area of headland, with high cliffs which jut out into the sea. It is well known because of the lighthouse which sits at the top of the cliffs. The waters around there are very deep and attract large marine species, such as sharks and dolphins.

Miranda and Sam arrived in the waters near Berry Head. Again they both heard a distant bellowing sound. They then swam due east, directly out to sea and towards the sound. After a while the bellowing sound became louder. They continued to swim in its direction. They knew that Bertram preferred the deep sea. Soon they saw an enormous blue shape in the water a short distance ahead.

'Hello, Sam and Your Ladyship. It is only your old friend Bertram,' he said.

'Welcome to the coast of South Devon, Bertram. It's great to see you. We have not seen you since last year,' responded Miranda.

'Well, you know me! I only pass this way once a year to see how you are. Lovely to see you, as always,' replied Bertram.

Bertram (or Bertie, as some called him) was a blue whale, the largest living mammal on earth. Blue whales live on plankton – microscopic organisms which live in the sea. Despite his enormous size, Bertram was a friendly whale and he enjoyed meeting his fellow inhabitants in the sea. His voice was very deep and he would sing whale songs to his fellow whales

across the vast expanse of the oceans.

Sam and Miranda told Bertram how they had been cleaning up the sea with the help of the crabs, and he was delighted. Even in the depths of the waters in the Arctic, rubbish from mankind was polluting the sea.

Bertram liked to go on tour in the summer months; he headed south to visit all of his friends in the northern seas. Miranda and Sam swam with him for another hour or so, exchanging gossip. He asked Miranda to give his best wishes to Gina and her newborn pup. South Devon was the most southerly point for Bertram on his travels. They parted company and he slowly headed back north to the ice-cold waters of the Arctic.

CHAPTER 6

A GATHERING

On a peaceful summer's evening Sam called round to meet Miranda. Tonight was the quarterly meeting of the South Devon Association of Seals. There was a thriving colony of grey seals in and around the port of Brixham, so the meeting was being held at St Mary's Bay, Brixham. Sam escorted Miranda to the meeting.

All of the seals in the area had gathered on the beach. Gina and her seal pup were there. The pup was no longer a ball of yellow fur – he had continued to put on weight and his fur had been replaced by a speckled grey-seal coat. All the seals welcomed the new pup. There were lots of other mothers there with their spring-born pups. Loving fathers and other relatives looked at them with pride.

The sun had gone down over the horizon, the sea was calm and waves gently lapped the shore. The bay was sheltered from the wind, and the nearby trees swayed in the soft breeze.

Sam introduced the Princess of the Sea as the chairperson, and the conference duly commenced.

'I wish to complain about the fishing trawlers fishing too far inshore and taking all of our food,' said little Tommy, an adolescent seal.

The seals clapped their front flippers in approval. Inshore fishing was a common complaint from the seals because their source of food was constantly being depleted.

'I would like to draw everyone's attention to a far greater threat – namely, getting caught up in the nets laid down by trawlers fishing in our traditional fishing grounds.' Old Charlie was a highly respected resident of Brixham Harbour.

A general discussion followed and everyone agreed with the complaints made by Tommy and Old Charlie. Miranda concluded matters at the meeting with the following summary.

'Thank you for coming. It's nice to see a full house. I appreciate the points you have raised and I give you every assurance that I will take the matter up with the Brixham Trawler Association. I am due to attend a meeting with them next week.'

It had been a tense meeting and Miranda and Sam were pleased it was over. Miranda had a good rapport with the fishermen of Brixham. Sam and Miranda discussed the points raised; Miranda told Sam that she felt confident that at the meeting the following week the fishermen would listen carefully and do their best to solve the seals' problems. She would also remind the fishermen that tourists enjoyed seal watching and they were a good attraction for visitors. Although Miranda was a mermaid she could talk like a human and she communicated well with the fishermen.

CHAPTER 7

A HOLIDAY INVITATION

The hot summer weather continued with long sunny days and endless blue skies. Miranda often went for a swim to enjoy the refreshing sea and meet her friends.

Miranda was sunbathing on the small platform of rock on one side of the Mewstone. She wore a large straw hat to keep the sun from her face. Sam was close by with his partner, Mary, and their young pup, Sheba. Sheba was fast asleep close to his mother.

Presently a seagull swooped down from the sky and landed by Miranda's tail. The seagull squawked a few times, dropped a note from his beak and then flew away. The seagull was Gertie, a tame gull that lived with Miranda's sister, Marianne. Sam sidled over to Miranda, keen to know the contents of the note. The note read as follows:

18 May 2019
The Haven,
Thatcher Rock,
Torquay,
Devon.

Dear Miranda,

The weather is lovely over here in Torquay. I have not seen you for a while and I hope you are well. Would you like to come and stay with me for a few days? My spare room is ready and you would be most welcome to come tomorrow.

Your loving sister,

Marianne

Miranda talked it over with Sam and she decided to go and stay with Marianne the following day. Marianne was a mermaid, the same as Miranda, and she was the guardian of the coastal waters around Torquay. She lived alone, with just Gertie as her faithful companion and messenger.

Marianne lived in a cave at the bottom of the sea on Thatcher Rock, near the coast at Torquay. Like the Mewstone, Thatcher Rock is a large island of rock protruding from the sea. Marianne's cave was much larger than Miranda's; she had two spacious bedrooms and a small third bedroom. She also had a tunnel leading from her cave upwards through the rock to the outside, where she had a flat rocky platform which she called her patio. During the warm summer months she spent most of her time on her island patio. She had spectacular views across the whole of Torbay and far out to sea, as well as overlooking Torquay.

CHAPTER 8

THATCHER ROCK

The following day Miranda swam from her home northwards towards Brixham. She rounded the massive headland of Berry Head. It was high summer. The tide was slack, and with her powerful mermaid tail she moved easily through the water.

From Berry Head she could have swum due north, direct to Thatcher Rock. However, she took a diversion west and headed inshore towards the shallow waters near Torre Abbey.

In the shallow waters near Torquay there is a large area of the seagrass *Zostera marina*. It stretches from near Torre Abbey southwards to Preston Sands. Miranda looked into the seagrass beds and soon saw the special creatures she had come to see. There were lots of them riding among the seagrass as it swayed in the current.

'Hello, Your Ladyship, and welcome to our home. My name is Neptune and I am head of our group,' said Neptune, the seahorse.

Neptune and his friends were very small – no more than about one inch long. Seahorses have an upright posture and their head is similar in shape to the head and neck of a horse. They have tiny gills of a delicate gossamer, which constantly flutter.

'Have you got everything you need for all of yourselves?' replied Miranda.

'Oh yes, we are quite happy here in the seagrass. It is a lot quieter now because no boats and fishing nets are allowed in our area, so we have it all to ourselves,' replied Neptune.

'Lovely to see you all, and best wishes,' said Miranda. 'I like to call in and see you when I travel on my way to see my sister, Marianne, at Thatcher Rock.'

Miranda then said goodbye to the little seahorses and headed east, out to sea and Thatcher Rock. The tide continued to be slack and she soon arrived at the rock. It was late afternoon and the sun was low in the sky – a golden orb of light casting rays of yellow light across the vast surface of the sea.

Marianne greeted her with a warm smile. She showed Miranda to her spacious bedroom complete with a shower room, a wardrobe and a large dressing table. Although the bedroom was in a cave under the sea, the room was well lit with candles.

Miranda joined her sister on the patio. The view of Torbay was breathtaking. She could see across the waters of Torbay and far out to sea, to the passing ships on the horizon.

They sat at a small table enjoying a cream tea with lashings of cream and jam. Gertie, the seagull, had kindly fetched the scones from a bakery near the clock tower on the quayside of Torquay.

Gertie was perched on her favourite rock close to Marianne. Above them, on the rocky crags of Thatcher Rock, a group of cormorants were resting, some with outstretched wings drying in the late afternoon sun. A flock of seagulls were circling in the sky, some diving into the sea to catch fish. In the sheltered waters of Torbay there was a dinghy race in progress – dinghies chasing after each other from buoy to buoy. The wind was light and it was perfect sailing weather for the evening races.

'Isn't it a beautiful afternoon?' said Marianne.

'It certainly is, with the evening sunshine and the dinghy racing,' replied Miranda.

'Yes, it is much busier here than back at the Mewstone,' said Miranda. She paused and then added, 'At the Mewstone I see a lot of yachts heading out to sea from the River Dart. I also get the occasional canoe party, who come to see the seals.'

Presently, in the water below them a grey seal popped his head out of the water. He had a mackerel in his mouth and was eating it, holding it tight with his front flippers. He stopped eating and gazed up at them.

'Afternoon, George,' said Marianne. 'This is my sister, Miranda – you know, the one I told you about. She is staying for a few days.'

'Welcome to Thatcher Rock, Miranda. I will catch some fish especially for you both,' replied George.

'He is a lovely old seal,' said Marianne. 'He calls on me most days for a chat.'

CHAPTER 9

PREPARATIONS

The hot summer weather continued unabated. Miranda was happy at her home on the Mewstone. It was mid-morning and Sam sidled along her hallway.

'Morning. Miranda. Just to let you know I can see Marianne and my old friend George approaching,' said Sam. 'I will escort them to the entrance to your home.'

'Thanks, Sam. You're an angel. Marianne is coming with me to the summer ball tonight and George is acting as our chaperone,' replied Miranda.

A short time later the two of them arrived. She had morning tea ready for them and plenty of fresh mackerel for George. They sat and chatted in the parlour.

'George, many thanks for being our chaperone,' said Miranda. She gave him a kiss on the cheek. She was sure she detected George was blushing.

'We met Sam's wife, Mary, and their pup, Sheba, on the way in. They are all excited about tonight's summer ball,' said Marianne.

'Yes, I know,' replied Miranda. 'We are going to swim with them to the ball tonight and all arrive together.'

It was early evening when Miranda and her party left the Mewstone and headed in a south-westerly direction towards Blackpool Sands. They arrived at the beach just as the sun was beginning to set. Miranda looked wonderful; her hair had been plaited and hung down the length of her back nearly to her waist. At the end of the plait she had tied a blue ribbon. She had cleaned and polished her mermaid tail and her scales sparkled emerald green.

Blackpool Sands is a magnificent beach of golden sand in a horseshoe shape on the coast of South Devon near Stoke Fleming. The cove is hemmed in on each side by rocky headlands. Behind the beach the land rises to low hills clad with conifer trees, and there are open fields with sheep and cattle. The beach is sheltered from the open sea, the water is crystal-clear and the waves gently lap the sandy shore.

CHAPTER 10

SUMMER BALL

It was now evening at Blackpool Sands. The sun was setting on the distant horizon. The sun glowed deep orange and the sea shimmered red, yellow and gold, with the rays of light spreading across the water.

Miranda, Marianne and George took up their spectator positions about fifty yards from the shore. Many marine creatures had arrived and others were on their way. Hundreds of pink crabs had gathered on the bottom of the sea. The seal colony from Brixham were lounging on the vast stretch of sandy beach. Mothers were with their pups of varying ages and their partners. Other grey seals were playing in the water.

Then a huge cheer came from the assembled throng to mark the arrival of Dolly the dolphin and Devon, her calf. In the excitement Dolly propelled herself out of the water. She did a spectacular leap through the air then hit the water, creating an enormous splash.

Then Miranda heard a little voice by her side: 'Good evening, Your Ladyship. It has taken me ages to get here from my little home at the Mewstone. I didn't want to miss the fun,' said Herman.

'Don't worry – the ball hasn't started just yet. You can come back with us – just hold on to the bow at the end of my hair,' replied Miranda.

The ball commenced with a line-dancing routine by the crabs. They had secretly been practising for the previous few weeks. They formed up in columns like a regiment. They formed lines with lady crabs on one side and gentlemen on the other. Their routine was intricate: they twirled round in unison, then partners held claws together and they performed a crab boogie-woogie. All the seals clapped their front flippers and cheered. At the end all of the crabs turned towards Miranda and did a little bow. Miranda, Marianne and George stood up and bowed low towards them as a mark of their appreciation.

The crabs then moved to the side of the bay to give centre stage to the seals. A group of about a dozen seals gathered on the surface of the sea and formed a large circle, touching each other, flipper to flipper. This was the beginning of their synchronised swimming routine.

Together, in unison, the seals dived down and performed a series of synchronised movements under the water. They did passing movements, underwater backflips, front rolls

and full body twists. They swished through the water with consummate ease. Their routine demonstrated their complete mastery of the marine environment.

At the end of their routine everyone cheered. The crabs clapped their claws and the seals clapped their flippers. Miranda and her party gave them a rousing round of applause.

The performing seals then swam ashore to join their friends and family on the beach. It was the biggest annual gathering of seals in Devon. The stage was then clear for the finale.

Dolly emerged from the western side of the cove. She raced through the water, performing a series of leaps. She moved at terrific speed. When she reached the centre of the bay she disappeared underwater for what seemed to be an eternity. She then leapt out of the water with tremendous force. She leapt very high into the air and dropped with barely a splash back into the sea.

Dolly continued her performance with a series of small leaps. She then commenced a series of medium-size leaps, forming a circle in the centre of the bay. For her finale she rejoined her calf, Devon, and together they did a lap of honour across the bay, swimming very close to the shore.

Everyone cheered and clapped flippers and claws in appreciation. Miranda, Marianne and George gave Dolly and Devon a standing ovation.